The Curious Incident of the Jam

An Olivia Bailey Baking Mystery

Written by Gail Lawler
Illustrations by Jane Burn

To Eliza,
With lots of love.
Your Cousin
Gail
xxxx

Olivia Jayne Bailey was not happy. She texted her friends with her elbows on the table, ignoring the sausages and toast set out before her. She wasn't in the least bit hungry and couldn't wait for her dad to go to work so that she could message her friends in peace. Her long, blonde hair fell across her face and hid one eye, the other fixed on her phone screen. Nothing was fair – she hated everything!

"Put your phone down when you're at the table, and eat your breakfast before it gets cold, Olivia." Her dad was firm but fair. He tried to make eye contact with his daughter, but it was impossible. She seemed impossible. Everything seemed such hard work with her at the moment, and he'd never felt so tired. That morning in the mirror, he'd noticed a few grey strands in his normally dark brown hair.

"But we always have sausages, dad! It was sausages yesterday and the day before that, and I hate sausages. Anyway, I'm not hungry."

Olivia let the fork she'd been clumsily holding slide onto the plate with a clatter.

"I'm not hungry."

Her blue eyes were defiant as she looked up at her dad, although secretly, she was on the verge of tears. Olivia was stubborn and wouldn't allow herself to cry. Not in front of her dad, anyway.

Joe Bailey's shoulders visibly drooped. A long day of work stretched before him, and all he wanted was a bit of peace and quiet. He was trying his best but was struggling to cope without his wife at home.

Jennifer Bailey was recovering well in hospital after an operation. Still, it would be another few weeks before she was allowed home. Father and daughter had been coping for just a few days, but the strain was already showing. It was only now that Joe Bailey truly appreciated his wife.

Looking across the table at his daughter, the long blonde hair hiding her sullen expression, he wondered where his real daughter had disappeared to. The one he used to know; the one that smiled and laughed at his jokes and would rush to the door to greet him with a big hug on his return home from work. The Olivia that liked him to read bedtime stories and didn't embarrass her.

Truth be told, he hardly saw his daughter these days. She was either at dancing or the local youth theatre in town. If not there, then she'd be at a friend's house or upstairs in her room, putting on make-up or chatting on her phone. It had been so different when he was young – no internet – no phones – just playing football outside with his friends in the fresh air. Things had seemed so much simpler then.

"Olivia?"

His voice was softer, eager to reconcile with his daughter as he reached his hand across the table to hers.

Olivia pulled her hand away quickly and stood up. Tears brimmed in her large blue eyes and clung to her dark eyelashes. Without speaking, she rushed out of the room and up to her bedroom, slamming the door shut behind her.

Joe Bailey's shoulders sagged a little more, and he sighed deeply. How on earth was he going to cope through the next few weeks without his wife? He'd barely lasted four days on his own. How had he become such a bad parent? He felt like an ogre out of one of the bedtime stories he'd read to Olivia when she was much younger.

The summer holidays had barely begun, and he had no idea what they could do? He wracked his brain for days out but had come up with a blank. He didn't even know what a twelve-year-old girl liked anymore. It would be easier to entertain an alien!

There was only one thing for it. He would ring his mother; she would know what to do.

Sue Bailey was what some people might call a free spirit, and she was more than happy with the label. She'd been a young, single mum, and Joe was her only child. They'd led a nomadic existence in his childhood. Had never had a permanent home, spending years with travelling groups or houses filled with families from diverse and interesting backgrounds.

Finally, she'd found her calling and settled down in the small village of Bampton, an ancient village lodged between two sloping valleys that were as old as time itself. Sue found herself drawn to the area and had never wanted to leave. The village boasted its own small stone circle- a mini Stonehenge, and the ancient mystic legends surrounding the magic hollow only increased its charm in her eyes. She'd started out by working in the local bakery. Twenty–five years later, she was now the proud owner of the 'Three Sisters' cafe- named after the small stone circle. Her home-baked delights proved a hit with the locals and tourists looking for enlightenment. Even if they didn't find the answer to the meaning of life, they could sit down and relax with a good strong coffee and a freshly baked jam and cream scone.

Sue Bailey was as well known in the village of Bampton as the Three Sisters themselves.

And she had an answer for every situation.

"Well, of course, why didn't you say something before Joe, my boy? Why didn't you phone me? There's only one thing for it; you must bring Olivia to stay with me until Jennifer is back home and well enough to cope. You know how I love to see my granddaughter- I see precious little of her these days."

It was true. Sue Bailey saw very little of her granddaughter, but it wasn't her fault. It had been fine up to a few years ago. Olivia had loved visiting her eccentric grandma, but somehow it wasn't cool at the age of twelve to make gingerbread men or even chocolate crispy buns.

Joe sighed. He could imagine poor Olivia's face when he told her she would have to stay with her grandmother for a few weeks. Still, it couldn't be worse than that morning had been, and it would give them both a bit of breathing space.

"OK, Mum. I'll bring her down at the weekend. See you then."

As Joe Bailey sank into a chair in part relief and part exhaustion, his mother was stirring into action almost fifty miles away.

"Now Tibby, my old boy, what's it to be? Caramel shortbread or chocolate brownies- which do you think she'll prefer?"

The large ginger tom cat blinked and yawned slowly. It was far too late for such questions. And curling up on a red embroidered cushion, he closed his eyes for a catnap.

"Well, you're no help, and that's for sure, Mr Tibbs," and shaking her head and laughing to herself, Sue Bailey started to bake.

Joe Bailey didn't underestimate his daughter's reaction to the news that she would spend most of the summer holidays with her gran in the sleepy village of Bampton. Yet, instead of screaming and shouting, she withdrew and refused to talk or even look at her father.

On Saturday morning, they set off quite early. Olivia spent the whole of the journey with her face turned away from her dad, looking out of the window and trying desperately to hold back the tears.

Everything was so horrible; she hated everything. She hated her dad for leaving her with her gran. She hated her mother for being ill. She hated her friends who would be spending the holidays together without her. But, more than any of that, she hated herself for feeling that way. She tried to reason that her mother was ill and that her father needed help, but it didn't make her feel any better. She just felt horrid.

And the more Olivia thought about her situation, the worse she felt. Her head became hot, and she could feel the anger inside her start to grow. She bit her lip to stop the tears from falling.

The car turned a corner, and a small sign announced the village of Bampton. Joe Bailey glanced across at his daughter sat by his side, and felt his stomach lurch. Was he doing the right thing?

The poor girl had hardly spoken to him since he'd told her the plan over breakfast a couple of mornings ago. She'd let her cornflakes go soggy in their bowl and ran to her room, slamming the door behind her and laid sobbing on the bed. He'd tried his best to talk to her, but it had been no use. The crying had eventually stopped, only to be replaced by a stony silence which was somehow much worse. Still, he had no choice, and it would only be for a few weeks. It really was for her own good, yet Joe Bailey couldn't help feeling that he'd betrayed his daughter; let her down somehow. He remembered the bedtime stories he'd read to her when she was a small girl. Knights in armour slaying a dragon or the prince saving the princess. Once he'd been all these things to his daughter, and now he couldn't even talk to her. Where had his little girl gone? It was almost as if she had disappeared only to be replaced by a moody goblin he no longer recognised.

The cottage cum cafe looked cheery and almost like out of a picture book itself. It boasted a thatch roof, and there was a neat cottage garden at the front where visitors could sit in the good weather to take their tea. The old Georgian window panes winked in the sunshine.

"Well, we're here, Olivia."

The girl continued to look out of the window at nothing in particular. No sooner had the car stopped, the cafe door was flung open, and there stood her grandma dressed in a brightly coloured kaftan and apron and beaming from ear to ear.

"Joe, Olivia- you're here at last."

Her hand was already tugging on the passenger door handle- eager to hug her granddaughter.

“Be nice to your grandma, Olivia.”

The girl managed to glare at her father, but before she had time to protest found herself being pulled from her seat and held against the substantial chest of her grandma.

“Why, Olivia, my love, how you’ve grown! Almost a young woman. Let me get a good look at you.”

The girl frowned heavily, her eyes red and thundery, but she did not speak.

“Now, why don’t you run inside, Olivia? I’ve made a fresh batch of cookies just for you. You can say hello to Mr Tibbs too.”

Olivia didn’t want a cookie. She wasn’t interested in the stupid old cat, either, but wanting to get away from the grown-ups, she did as she was told.

“I’m sorry about Olivia. I don’t know what’s got into her lately?” Joe looked up at his mother apologetically.

Sue smiled fondly at her son. He looked tired, but it didn’t seem that long ago since he was a young boy himself.

“Now, don’t you worry about her, son. She will be just fine. I promise. It’s hard on a girl of her age not to have her mum around. I suppose her old eccentric grandma isn’t much of a substitute - but she’ll be fine- I promise you. You have to remember Olivia is at a sensitive age. Growing up’s not easy - I remember you at that age!”

Joe opened his mouth to protest – surely he hadn’t been any trouble as a boy? But before he could speak, his mother grabbed him by the arm and started pulling him toward the house.

“Now leave her with me and stop worrying. You have enough on your plate with Jennifer in the hospital. Now come and have a cuppa before you drive back home.”

THREE SISTERS' CAFÉ
5

Olivia made her way up the windy old staircase at the back of the cafe to the living quarters above. She'd always loved the rickety old house when she was younger, but now it seemed small and old, and she could only view it as a prison for the next few weeks. Halfway up the stairs, the cat appeared out of nowhere and started to wind itself through her legs - almost tripping her up.

With a sharp tap of her foot, she attempted to kick it aside, but the nimble old moggy pranced daintily out of the way and back down the staircase.

"Stupid old cat," Olivia muttered under her breath and, climbing the remaining stairs, eventually made it to the top floor. The bedroom hidden away in the attic, under the eaves, had always been hers whenever she stayed there.

In fact, it had been several years since Olivia had slept in her old room. She'd visited her grandma, of course, but had grown out of wanting to stay overnight.

Seeing the old room again, with the small reminders of years gone by, caused a stab at her heart, but Olivia wasn't sure why.

Everything was as she remembered - the patchwork coverlet and the old rag doll abandoned for years- waiting for someone to play with. Olivia picked up the cloth doll and cradled it in her arms; she hadn't played with dolls for years now. Her iPhone and TickTock took up most of her time these days, yet something was reassuring about the old doll. She carefully traced the faded stitching with her fingers and found it oddly comforting. Soon Olivia found herself sitting on the bed, sobbing into the little cloth face and feeling extremely sorry for herself.

"Oh, Emily. It's not fair. It's the holidays, and I'm stuck here with Grandma. There's no wifi, and you're my only playmate."

The little doll looked back with its large blue, cloth eyes but said nothing.

A car started up outside - her father was leaving.

Rushing to the window, Olivia gazed sadly at the departing car.

"He didn't even say goodbye, Emily."

And with a stamp of her foot, Olivia threw the little doll to the foot of the bed.

"Stupid doll."

Sue Bailey called up the stairs several times to her granddaughter- but after being met by silence, decided to walk up the two flights of stairs to speak face to face with the young girl.

After a brief knock, she entered the room, carrying a tray of cookies and a glass of milk.

"I thought you might like these, sweetheart?"

Placing the tray on the dressing table, Sue sat beside her granddaughter on the bed, ready for a *'woman to woman'* chat.

"Your father's gone back home now Olivia, I thought it might be better for you that way. No tearful goodbyes, eh?"

Olivia looked at her hands.

"He really does love you, you know."

Olivia fought to keep away the tears. She was determined not to cry in front of her grandma.

After several more minutes of silence, Sue stood and made her way to the door. There would be plenty of time to talk when Olivia had settled in.

"Well, I'll leave you with the milk and cookies, love. Come down when you're ready. There's no rush."

Patting the young girl gently on the shoulder, Sue silently left the room.

Her son had been such a happy child. He'd given her no cause for worry growing up. Maybe the odd scrapes when a teenager. Joe had always been out playing. He'd been such an imaginative child, making up games when there was no one to play with. Times were different now. It seemed no longer safe for kids to play out on the street, although she often wondered if that was really the case. Times were definitely different. With the onset of computer games and the like, children didn't seem to play outside anymore. The old traditional games of *'tag'* and *'hide and seek'* she'd played as a girl were dying out - like something only seen in a museum.

Of course, times had to change. That was progress, wasn't it? Her own childhood had been a world away from her son's. The 1960s had been rather a strict time for parenting, at least in her family. Children had been seen but not heard. The swinging sixties had been an alien concept to her parents, more distant than computers and technology were to her generation today. Sue had reacted by rebelling and running away from home at sixteen.

She was determined to do better with her own grandchild. Once they'd been close, but Olivia was becoming a young woman and was no longer a child.

Sue's shoulders sagged; she probably had as much in common with her granddaughter as her parents had with her.

Mr Tibbs sidled past her on the stairs and gave a tiny meow. He always could tell when something was wrong.

"Oh, Mr Tibbs – what am I going to do?"

The old cat blinked back with wise green eyes.

Despite her mood, Olivia started to feel hungry. As usual, she'd eaten very little breakfast, and the waft of homemade cookies was too tempting, and the sweet smell of vanilla and melted chocolate was irresistible. Olivia had almost forgotten what a good baker her grandma was.

One delicious biscuit followed another and another, and soon they were all gone. The glass of milk washed them down nicely.

The sugar improved her mood slightly; she was always a little out of sorts when hungry, and sitting back on the bed allowed her head to fall back onto the pillow, and she closed her eyes.

The afternoon sun streaming in through the window warmed her face, and she began to doze. The emotions of the last few days had worn her out, and all she wanted to do was rest, the old cottage lulling her to sleep, whispering its secrets as she slept.

The brush of fur against her legs awoke Olivia with a start.

"Mr Tibbs- get down."

The old cat purred and padded across the bed and looked deeply into her eyes.

Meoooow.

Olivia laughed and rubbed the furry head. She had grown up with Mr Tibbs and played with him since he was a kitten.

"It looks like you're my only friend for the holidays, Tibby."

The old cat blinked back but said nothing.

The afternoon sun poured into the room. It seemed much smaller than Olivia had remembered; she hadn't really given the place a second thought until now. She'd spent many happy weekends here with her grandma while her mum and dad had been away. Playing in the pretty cottage garden and helping in the cafe, baking delicious goodies. They'd been happy times- but of course, she'd only been a 'kid' then. When she was seven or eight, those activities had been OK, but now she was grown up, she didn't 'play' anymore. Instead, she listened to music and painted her fingernails. She went to a dancing class twice a week, and afterwards, her gang went to McDonald's for chips. She had her own spending money and was allowed to buy her own clothes.

Olivia sighed at the thought of the school holidays looming ahead. Weeks without her friends- she couldn't even contact them on Facebook or even post videos on TikTok. There was no wifi connection here and no phone signal either. Her grandma had been adamant that the café would be free from mobile phones and such interruptions. There was even a sign displayed in the tea room that read:

"We do not have WIFI – Talk to each other and enjoy the view instead."

It was so unfair.

The room had never changed. Olivia stood and walked over to the old mantelpiece and picked up a small ornament, and twisted it around in her fingers. It was an old pot dog with a missing ear. She had bought it from a local jumble sale when she was just six years old. Olivia had felt sorry for the poor thing and had paid just a few pence for it. Looking at it now made her feel sad, and she wondered why.

An old gold-coloured clock ticked gently by its side. The pretty dial was painted with flowers, and she watched the second hand on its slow rotation around the face. Each unit of time measured precisely, never too fast and never too slow; constant and unstoppable.

An old bookcase stood in one corner of the room, and she ran her fingers across the old battered spines; these were some of her favourite childhood stories. Her grandma had often read her a bedtime tale, even when she could read for herself. Sue brought the stories to life with her silly voices and theatrics.

Olivia pulled out a large illustrated book; it had been one of her favourites- *Alice's Adventures in Wonderland.* Sitting on the bed, she let the pages fall open and lost herself in the magic for a while, the illustrations casting a spell over her gloom. The book was quite old, and the pages were delicate and worn through years of use.

The forgotten Mr Tibbs purred gently against her legs.

"Oh Tibby, it's a fine book, but so babyish now. It was OK when I was little, but now I'm almost a teenager."

Flinging the book across the duvet, it slid with a thump and crashed to the floor- splitting the spine and severing the frail old book into two.

"Oh!"

Olivia rushed to pick up the pieces, feeling immediately sorry for the old book.

Holding the two halves in each hand, she inspected the damage. The spine had ripped clean away, and several pages were now falling out. Olivia tried to piece it back together using her hands, but it was pretty hopeless. The old book was beyond repair.

Placing the fragments onto the bed, Olivia could feel the tears welling in her eyes again. Sensing her unhappiness, the old cat jumped up and into her arms.

"Oh, Mr Tibbs- everything is going wrong lately- what shall I do?"

For a while, she stood looking at the torn pages of the book, the warmth and softness of the cat offering some small comfort.

A sheet had ripped away from the inside front cover of the book. It had obviously been stuck over the original, and Olivia could see some faded writing beneath.

Examining it more closely, Olivia saw that something had been written in a rather bold and looping hand. She had seen writing like it in the history books they studied at school.

It was an inscription of some sort, but half of the writing was still covered by the torn paper. Tugging very gently at the remaining paper, Olivia peeled it back to reveal the words. She was rather excited- it was like uncovering a lost secret from the past.

At first, the writing was difficult to read – the writing style almost making it look like a foreign language, like something from the French she'd just started to study. But it wasn't French or any other language- it was English, and slowly, the words made sense.

Presented to Mary Anne Nicholls on the occasion of her being crowned May Queen on the first of May in the year of our Lord 1898.

1898. Olivia's eyes widened; that was over 120 years ago. Running her fingers over the beautiful inked letters, she wondered who Mary Anne Nicholls was. She imagined a young girl, very much like herself but dressed in Victorian clothing. Her class had studied the Victorian era at school, and she'd been fascinated. She often told her mother that she would like to travel back in time and be a Victorian schoolgirl. Her mother only laughed and reminded her that the Victorians didn't have internet or mobile phones and Facebook. Instead, young girls had to help their mothers with household chores- manual work with no electricity.

Olivia caught herself in the old mirror, one of three that stood on the old dressing table. Three Olivia's looked back at her from different angles, almost as if three different girls were looking at her. It was funny. Sometimes she felt like three totally different girls and was full of contradictions. She loved the modern world and technology, but she also felt nostalgic for the past- for things she read in history books at school. Sometimes she was happy with her life, and sometimes she hated everything. She'd almost forgotten this part of herself, but the old room was bringing it all back. She wanted desperately to be happy, but these days she often felt sad- for no reason at all. Her mother had told her that it was just part of growing up, but she would rather stay a child if that was what growing up meant. But then her other self loved being grown up, buying clothes, and listening to music. It was almost as if half of her wanted to remain a child and the other half be grown up.

Olivia was torn between two worlds, the old and the new, making her feel funny inside. Sometimes life was so confusing.

"Olivia, Olivia, it's tea time – are you ready?"

Her gran's voice filtered up the two flights of stairs. Olivia glanced at the clock; already six 'o'clock. Time either went too slow or too fast these days; something else that puzzled her. The cafe had already been closed for an hour; she must have slept for longer than she thought.

There was a delicious smell in the kitchen, roast chicken and vegetables- usually Olivia's favourite, but suddenly she didn't feel hungry. On the table stood a whole tray of freshly baked strawberry jam tarts that had been cooked in Olivia's honour. The jam was still bubbling within the golden pastry casing. Even they didn't make her feel happy. All that thinking had churned her up inside.

"How are you feeling now, love?"

She didn't really want to talk to her grandma either. It was almost as if she were a stranger. It had been different when she was younger; she'd chatted easily to her grandma about this and that. But these days, her thoughts were much more personal and private. How could her gran possibly understand what she was thinking?

Sue Bailey felt a slight tug at her heart as she watched Olivia push the food disinterestedly around her plate. What had happened to the happy, go-lucky child of just a few years ago? At her age, she too had been unhappy, but for other reasons. She would have never dared leave any food; rationing after the second world war was still clearly imprinted in her parent's minds. The 1960s were in full swing, her friends were wearing black eyeliner and miniskirts, and she was allowed neither. She wasn't even allowed to play records or have friends to tea. Olivia had a lot to be grateful for. Still, each generation had its own worries and constraints, however liberal they might seem to the previous generation.

The meal passed by in relative silence, both parties lost in their own thoughts. It was only the distant crying of Mr Tibbs that broke the spell.

"Oh poor Mr Tibbs, I'd quite forgot about his dinner. Olivia, would you be a dear and go and see to him?"

Relieved to have an excuse to leave the table, Olivia quickly headed for the door to the kitchen.

"Olivia?"

Her Grandmother's voice was soft and low, and the girl stopped in her tracks, the door half-open.

"We do love you, you know."

Olivia left quickly in silence.

The girl lay on her bed. Without her tablet or phone, she was bored and didn't know what to do with herself. She'd read all the books on the bookshelf several times over, and besides, she was too old for them now. She wondered if she should mention the broken book to her grandma but decided to put it back onto the bookshelf. No one would bother with it, so why make a fuss.

Stooping to the floor, she picked up a stray page that must have fallen from the torn book earlier. On it was one of her favourite illustrations – The Knave of Hearts on trial for stealing the Queen's Jam tarts.

"The Queen of Hearts, she made some tarts,
All on a summer day:
The Knave of Hearts, he stole those tarts,
And took them quite away!"

Olivia thought about the jam tarts on the table downstairs and immediately felt hungry, having eaten very little dinner. She could almost taste the crisp butter pastry and sweet fragrant strawberry jam. But that would mean going into the kitchen where her gran would try and make conversation again.

Instead, she lay back on the bed and closed her eyes, trying to forget the rumbling in her tummy.

The night was long and impatient. The rafters of the old cottage sighed and groaned as the wind began to blow through the ancient timbers, disturbing sleeping ghosts and forgotten memories lost among the dust and debris. Sleep was restless and fitful, filled with dark and shadowy dreams.

Olivia awoke with a start. She thought she heard a noise but listened carefully for several minutes. All was quiet except for the steady rhythm of the ticking clock - like a tiny beating heart,

She peered through the gloom. It was 5:30 am and almost dawn. She must have slept all through the night. But what had awoken her so early?

Straining her ears, she listened carefully. There it was again- the distant strains of music coming from outside; she was sure of it.

Quickly jumping from the bed, Olivia rushed over to the window and drew back the curtains. The early mist was rising over the fields beyond the cafe. The stone circle stood atop a small mound in the distance, and through the emerging morning light, it looked quite mystical.

There seemed to be something happening amongst the ancient stones. Olivia screwed her eyes up tightly and tried to focus on the moving shapes.

At first, she saw one figure emerge from behind the stones, then another and another. It seemed to be a small band of some sort, and they all seemed to be playing musical instruments, although Olivia couldn't see quite what. The music was like nothing she'd ever heard, almost like fairy playing- a light and sweet melody that seemed distant and yet all around her. The figures appeared to be in fancy dress, some wearing long cloaks and others wearing animal masks. She could definitely see a pair of large ears and a long tail.

Olivia was intrigued. Maybe it was the local Morris Men or something like that. She'd seen them dancing on May Day back home, celebrating the spring, and also something called the Mummers play at Christmas, where someone dressed up as the devil and one man as a woman and one as a sheep. She hadn't understood the play, but it had been quite funny. Yes, she thought- it must be them. Despite the early hour, Olivia decided to get dressed and venture outside to see for herself. Her grandma had let her play out on her own from a young age. Anyhow, the music seemed so gentle and melodic that she felt comforted by it.

The old stairs were creaky, and Olivia stopped halfway down to listen in case the music had awoken her grandma. The old house whispered and rattled around her, but the gentle snoring coming from the first-floor bedroom indicated that her grandma was well and truly asleep. Only Mr Tibbs was awake; not much got past the old cat, and either hearing or sensing the girl, he sprang quietly up the stairs to where she was standing.

"Be quiet, Tibby," she whispered, holding a finger to her lips as if the puss would understand. Noiselessly he rubbed against her legs, and together the two tiptoed silently down the stairs so as not to wake the sleeping woman.

As they reached the kitchen door, Olivia's stomach let out a growl.

"Oh Tibby, I'm so hungry- I hardly ate a thing yesterday apart from the milk and cookies. I'm sure Grandma won't mind if I sneak a few of the jam tarts and take them with me for breakfast."

Olivia walked across the cold kitchen floor and looked at the table. Where there had been a dozen jam tarts – now were two, with only a few crumbs to show where the remaining tarts had been.

Scratching her head, the girl turned to face the cat.

"Where on earth have all the tarts gone, Tibby? Surely Grandma hasn't eaten them all by herself?"

The cat raised an eyebrow.

"Yes, your right, Tibby. Grandma Sue does have a very sweet tooth, but even she couldn't eat ten strawberry jam tarts – of that, I'm certain. Still, I'm so hungry I must take the remaining two. I'm sure she won't mind. They were baked for me, after all."

Stuffing one tart into her mouth and one in her pocket for later, Olivia stepped out through the hallway.

The door was unlocked. In this small hamlet, there was no need to lock doors. Everyone knew each other, and neighbours kept a watchful eye, and little went undetected.

The air was still fresh, and the cat lifted his pink nose into the air as though sensing something in the easterly breeze.

It was quite a steep climb to the small stone circle, up a winding track that had been worn into the hillside by the countless pilgrims treading the ancient way. Olivia wrapped the old coat tightly around her. She had grabbed the nearest thing on her way out and only realised now that it was her gran's old woollen coat. It smelled sweet, a fragrant imprint of the owner- a mixture of earthy patchouli and amber – and baking, of course.

The old cat trotted behind her.

"Go back, Tibby; I don't want you getting lost."

Yet the old cat didn't leave her side and instead gave her a knowing look with its wise green eyes.

The music grew louder as the two approached the stones which lay a short distance ahead, just beyond a thicket of trees.

"Wait here a moment, Tibby, and I'll try and get a better look at what's happening."

As if understanding, the cat stood quite still as Olivia approached the trees. Hiding beneath the boughs, she peered through the foliage.

She could see the figures quite clearly from her viewpoint and what a queer picture they made. Ahead of her was a procession; men and women dressed in elaborate costumes and slowly dancing around the stone circle. There was a giant rabbit and a frog, and even a horse. Olivia wondered where they got the outfits from. One character wearing a giant dog's head started to beat loudly on a small drum he carried around his neck.

"STOP."

A loud female voice boomed from the front of the group, and the procession halted immediately.

"There is a stranger in our midst."

Olivia felt the hairs stand up on the back of her neck. She couldn't see the speaker of the deep and booming voice, but maybe the speaker could see her? The strange crowd parted as the figure came into view.

It was an older woman with a highly made-up face. She looked like something from a pantomime, thought Olivia. Two large red spots were circled around her cheeks, and the rest of her face was painted white, with the mouth and eyes painted heavily – almost like a clown. On the top of her head, she wore a crown made of blossom-which looked quite ridiculous on such a grotesque figure.

All eyes were now upon the thicket of trees where Olivia was standing. No-one moved. Holding her breath, the girl stood as still and as quiet as possible. Hopefully, they would lose interest and move on.

Just as it looked as though the procession would continue, Mr Tibbs decided to pounce towards a rather large and vicious-looking figure of a mouse.

"Mr Tibbs!"

Olivia tried to shout the cat back as quietly as she could, but it was too late-all eyes were upon the cat who sat hissing at the mouse-like creature.

"Who's there?" The large female demanded, pointing directly towards poor Mr Tibbs.

At first, Olivia feared for the old cat, but to her surprise, the old feline stood up on his back legs and approached the woman as if he were human himself.

"Excuse me(ow), your Majesty. I couldn't help my natural instincts, and the sight of my good lady Mouse here stirred something within me. I do most humbly beg your pardon."

Olivia clung onto the tree, almost falling over from the shock of seeing and hearing Mr Tibbs walking and speaking. She noticed that his hackles were raised-the fur standing upright on the back of his neck. He always did that when he felt threatened.

"Ah, it is you, Mr Tibbs, Sir. You know it is in extremely bad taste to let one's natural instincts get the better of one. We are not animals, you know."

The cat gave a low and very solemn bow.

"Forgive me (ow), your Majesty. It is early in the morning, and I have not yet had my breakfast."

The old face looked angry, even angrier than it had before. And that was no mean feat!

"Breakfast, BREAKFAST- how dare you talk about breakfast to me, you mangy bit of fur. I have not yet had my breakfast- someone has STOLEN my breakfast. We are now looking for the culprit. Perhaps it is YOU that has stolen MY BREAKFAST?"

The old cat looked perplexed.

"I have no idea what you are talking about, your Majesty. I have not even seen BREAKFAST this morning and wouldn't know what it looked like even if I had seen it?"

"Impertinent Moggie, how dare you talk to me like that? Someone has stolen the jam tarts, MY jam tarts, and that is a punishable offence, as well you know."

The cat began to back away.

"I am truly sorry for your cat-astrophe, your Majesty. But I know nothing about strawberry jam tarts. Now, if that is all, I will be on my way. Things to do and people to see, you know?"

The old woman's eyes narrowed.

"How did you know that they were STRAWBERRY jam tarts? You would only know that if you had STOLEN them – seize him, guards."

Before the poor cat could continue, two giant white rabbits wearing elaborate uniforms and carrying ceremonial weapons walked forward.

"If you would be so kind as to accompany us to the Royal Court, Sir," they said, roughly taking hold of poor old Mr Tibbs by his two front paws.

Olivia, who had been quietly watching the scene from behind the trees, could no longer be quiet. She had to save poor Mr Tibbs. Without thinking of herself, she rushed forward in defence of the poor cat.

"STOP!"

Olivia shouted loudly as the guards began to lead the cat away.

Immediately they stopped and looked around, not quite sure what to do next. In fact, they didn't know if they were coming or going, or both?

"Who demands us to STOP?"

The deep female voice boomed across to where Olivia was standing.

"I do," answered Olivia, rather meekly.

"Mr Tibbs did not steal your jam tarts; you must let him go immediately."

The old woman raised an eyebrow.

"If Mr Tibbs is not the thief, then how did he know that the tarts were strawberry flavoured?" demanded the Queen.

"Aren't all tarts strawberry? commanded Olivia. "All the tarts I have ever eaten have been strawberry."

The old woman looked shocked.

"Impertinent child. How dare you answer me back. What is your name, and who are you?" demanded the painted face.

"I am Olivia Jayne, and that is my name, and my name is also who I am. Isn't that the same thing? Who are you?"

The group that had now gathered around her gasped. No one had ever spoken to their Queen like that before. No one had ever dared.

"Go back, Olivia." Mr Tibbs shouted, but it was too late.

"I, Olivia Jayne, am the May Queen, but that does not mean I am Queen of the May?"

"But that doesn't make any sense whatsoever," said Olivia. "That is plain nonsense."

The Queen's eyes were stormy as she approached the young girl, the bulky form towering high above the young girl's head.

Olivia looked puzzled.

"Anyway, aren't you a bit old to be the May Queen?"

Olivia had always been brought up to tell the truth. She didn't mean to sound rude, but the words had been on the tip of her tongue and somehow slipped out.

The crowd now held their collective breath, and someone dressed as a small mole fainted clean away.

The old May Queen looked as if she were about to choke. Her eyes bulged, and her brightly rouged cheeks grew redder by the minute as if she was about to burst.

"How very dare you. I have never heard anything so impertinent in all my life. I am as young as my toes and a little bit older than my teeth – that is all. Now, guards- arrest this girl for speaking the truth."

How ridiculous, thought Olivia. Being arrested for speaking the truth. What an upside-down sort of justice that seemed to be.

Although she dodged the white rabbits, the quick and cunning mouse caught her by the arm and held her quite firmly until she could be handed over to the guards.

As she struggled to escape, something fell out of her pocket.

"Well, well. What have we here?"

The mouse bent down and picked up the strawberry jam tart that had been concealed in her pocket and had been saving for breakfast.

The May Queen smiled sadistically.

"So it is you. You are the thief that stole my strawberry jam tarts. The one who talks in riddles is the girl who stole the tarts."

Olivia stomped her foot defiantly on the hard ground.

"I did not steal your strawberry jam tarts; in fact, someone has stolen my GRANDMA'S jam tarts. She made twelve of them yesterday and left them on the kitchen table last night, and this morning there were only two."

The Queen narrowed her eyes again.

"So if there were two left, where is the other tart?"

The strange group of creatures gathered around her, their voices whispering low accusations.

Olivia began to feel slightly nervous.

"Why I ate it, of course!"

For a moment, there was silence. Then one by one, the voices around her started muttering in unison.

"Why she ate it, of course, she ate it, of course, why she ate it, of course."

"QUIET."

The old Queen boomed across the heads of the assorted creatures. Immediately there was silence.

"This is a most serious matter, a matter that requires the court to make a sentence. Let the court begin!"

Olivia was led into the middle of the circle of stones. Upon one of the slabs was mounted a great throne on which the Queen sat. She was now wearing a preposterous wig- on top of which perched the May blossom crown, which looked even more ridiculous.

"Are YOU to be my judge?" Olivia asked in surprise, for she had never heard of a Queen being a judge before.

The old head nodded.

"So, who will be my jury?" Olivia wasn't too sure what a jury was but had heard the term on TV.

"We will be the Jury." Twelve of the assorted creatures, both birds and beasts, stepped forward and proceeded to sit on twelve ornate chairs placed to the right of the Queen.

"Now, who will read out the sentence?" the Queen demanded.

"I will." It was Mr Tibbs. He was now dressed in a bowler hat and a rather splendid yellow waistcoat. Around his neck, he sported a gold chain, and on the end of the chain was a gold watch with a beautifully painted face. It looked the same as the clock in her bedroom back at grandma's house– but how could that be? She could hear the gentle tick, tick of the clock as the second hand raced around the dial.

The minute and the hour hand were both pointing upright.

"12 o'clock. It can't be?" Olivia spoke aloud. I've only been away from the house for half an hour at most. It can't be 12 o'clock already!"

As she glanced at the watch, the second hand seemed to be moving much quicker than usual.

"Actually, you're quite right, Olivia. It isn't 12 o'clock at all. It's now 2 o'clock." Mr Tibbs tapped at the glass on the front of his watch and nodded in agreement with his own statement.

"But it was only 12 o'clock a minute ago! I have never known time to fly so quickly. This is most strange," muttered Olivia.

"You are, in fact, late, Olivia; late for your own trial. That will go against you in court," one of the White Rabbits solemnly pointed out.

"Silence." The May Queen held up her arms.

"This court is now in session. We will hear the sentence, Mr Tibbs."

The ginger tom cat produced a large scroll from within his waistcoat and proceeded to unroll it as the White Rabbits began to blow on their trumpets.

The old cat cleared his throat with a loud harrumph before proceeding.

"The May Queen against Olivia. The sentence is..."

At this point, the old cat stopped.

"What is the matter, Tibbs" the old Queen boomed.

The cat looked over the half-rimmed spectacles he was now wearing.

"I was merely '***pawsing*** for effect,' your honour."

The jury began to clap, and someone held up a small placard. Mr Tibbs had scored 8 out of 10 for his joke.

"Get on with it, Tibbs. Read out the sentence." The May Queen bawled.

The cat cleared his throat again.

"The sentence is, the sentence is... My name is also who I am. Isn't that the same thing?"

The jury began to clap and nod again, repeating the sentence.

"My name is also who I am. Isn't that the same thing? My name is also who I am. Isn't that the same thing?"

The jury huddled together, and after much prevarication and scribbling, a mouse stepped forward and held up a card. The sentence had scored a perfect 10.

"Overruled. That sentence doesn't make sense." The May Queen scowled at the jury, who sat quickly back down in their places,

"Who will speak for the defendant?"

The Queen looked angry.

No one stepped forward.

"Is there anyone who will speak on behalf of the defendant?"

"I can speak perfectly well for myself."Olivia took two steps towards the Queen.

"This is most irregular; most irregular indeed. But very well, what do you have to say in your defence?"

"All I can say is that I did not steal ***YOUR*** jam tarts. Those tarts belonged to ***ME*** and were made by my Grandmother. Someone has stolen ***MY*** jam tarts, and I am the victim as much as you are. There is obviously someone going around stealing jam tarts, and we are both the victims."

The jury started to clap again but were soon silenced by a wave of the Queen's hand.

"But what about the sentence? When we have heard your defence of the sentence, we can eat the jam tarts and go home to bed."

Olivia looked puzzled.

"But I'm not sure what the sentence is?"

The May Queen sighed and looked across to Mr Tibbs, who was now lying on the grass and enjoying the sunshine, wearing a huge pair of sunglasses.

"Tibbs, the sentence again, if you would be so kind?"

Yawning, the cat lazily pulled the scroll out of his waistcoat once more (that was now rather untidily unbuttoned) and proceeded to read out the sentence again.

"My name is also who I am. Isn't that the same thing?"

Olivia scratched her head.

"But that doesn't make sense?"

"Exactly, but that is what you said, so what do you have to say in your defence?"

"No. No! It's not that the sentence doesn't make sense. It's the fact that I have to defend the sentence? I thought I was on trial for the theft of jam tarts?"

"JAM TARTS?" the May Queen looked amused and started to laugh. "Why on earth would this be about Jam Tarts, Olivia?"

The jury began to clap and laugh until the whole court was in an uproar.

"This is the most ridiculous thing that I have ever heard!" Olivia was beginning to feel rather angry and wished she were back home in bed.

Just at that moment, one of the White Rabbits stood up and, raising his trumpet, started to play a herald – announcing the Knave of Hearts.

A young man, dressed in a rather fetching outfit covered in red hearts, strode forward carrying a plate of strawberry jam tarts. Olivia counted quickly. There were ten.

"Jam tarts, your majesty." The Royal Knave gave a long low bow and presented the delicacies to the May Queen, who smiled graciously across to Olivia.

"It is quite simple, Olivia. If you put up your defence against the sentence, the sooner the jury can decide. Then we can eat the jam tarts and all go home. Now, what is your defence?"

"About the sentence?"

"Yes, about the sentence. We have already established that my son has stolen the tarts. He does that from time to time. Now they are returned, we can carry on with the sentence."

The May Queen was now starting to feel quite weary, and her shoulders sagged.

"Come along, girl."

"Well," stammered Olivia.

"WELL," stammered back the jury in unison before sitting in silence and waiting for the response.

"Actually, it's all very simple," Olivia stated boldly, even though her knees were feeling rather trembly. She looked around for her feline friend, but Mr Tibbs had already lost interest in the whole thing and was laid amongst the grass with his eyes closed.

"Well. You see, you asked me my name and who I was, and I replied My name is Olivia Jayne, and my name is also who I am. Isn't that the same thing? I meant that I am called Olivia Jayne, that's all, and then I asked who you were."

The old May Queen looked perplexed.

"I am the May Queen. That is who I am," stated the May Queen rather forcefully. "Let that be an end to it."

"But haven't you got a name?" asked Olivia, who was also getting rather tired of the game.

"Like what?" asked the Queen

"Well, like Olivia, I suppose?"

The old Queen scratched her head. "I am sure that I would have known if I were an Olivia. I am sure that I would FEEL it somehow. No, I am definitely not an Olivia. Mr Tibbs, fetch me my BOOK."

The poor old cat had been dreaming a jolly nice sort of dream about catching giant mice and didn't care to be woken.

"Mr Tibbs, if you please." The old May Queen shouted, somewhat irritated.

Fastening his waistcoat, the old cat walked over to one of the three large standing stones and drew out a battered old leather satchel from behind it. Opening it up, he pulled out a book and presented it to the Queen.

"Your book, your majesty." And giving a quick bow, he returned to his slumber in the long grass.

As the May Queen opened the first page of the book, Olivia gave a gasp of recognition. It was the old book from her room, the one that had fallen apart.

"My name is Mary Anne Nicholls" the Queen smiled triumphantly. "That is my name, and that is who I am."

Olivia could feel her temper start to rise.

"That is not your book, and that is not your name. That book belongs to my Grandma. It is a very old book, and it broke in two earlier today. Now please give it back to me".

The May Queen picked up the book and held it high in the air. It was quite complete and looked brand new.

"I'm afraid you are wrong, my dear. I can assure you that this is my name and that this is my book."

Olivia could see that the book was now in one piece but knew the book was hers.

"I'm not sure what trick you are playing on me, but that is not your name and NOT your book. Now please return it to me."

The Queen smiled, her face almost splitting with the effort.

"But my dear, if this is not my book and not my name, then who am I?"

The young girl thought hard for a moment.

"Well, if you do not have a name, then I'm afraid that you are no one and do not, in fact, exist."

All at once, the jury rose to their feet, clapping their hands and stamping their feet.

"The Queen does not exist, the Queen does not exist," they all shouted.

They chanted over and over again.

“Stop this nonsense at once,” the May Queen waved her hands for the others to be quiet. But as she no longer existed, they could no longer hear her. The more they chanted, the fainter and fainter the old Queen became until she had entirely faded away.

“If there’s no judge, what happens to the court” shouted the small mole that had fainted earlier and was quite relieved to see the bad-tempered Old May Queen disappear.

“I’m afraid in this case, the court is adjourned, and the case dismissed,” shouted a white rabbit, and everyone cheered.

And with that, Mr Tibbs picked up one of the drums and started beating it. As he did so, one by one, the jury disappeared. First, the horse and the white rabbits, then the dog, the mouse, and mole, until all the animals had vanished into thin air.

Olivia gazed in astonishment until she was the only one left standing alone in the middle of the stone circle.

“Mr Tibbs, what has happened? Where did they all go?”

Looking around, she searched for the old ginger tomcat, but he was nowhere to be seen. It was only when she felt something soft brush against her that she looked down, and there, on all fours again, was Mr Tibbs rubbing against her legs.

“Oh, Tibby, what’s been going on?”

The old cat blinked back through his green eyes.

Meow.

What a queer adventure, Olivia thought. She suddenly felt exhausted and longed to be back in her bed.

“C’mon Tibbs, we better head back. Gran might be worried about us,” and the girl and cat set back down the hill once again towards the little cafe.

The strange thing was that when Olivia arrived back home, it was only 6 o’clock in the morning. Only half an hour had passed since she’d left the house. Tiptoeing back up the stairs, she paused on the landing and listened. Her grandma was still soundly asleep and snoring away.

Olivia, too, felt the need to sleep. After the events of the morning, she was exhausted.

Soon she was back in bed sleeping soundly with Mr Tibbs curled up at the foot of her bed.

It was 10 o'clock in the morning when Olivia was finally awoken by her grandma carrying a breakfast tray of tea and toast into her room.

"You've had a long sleep Olivia, how are you feeling this morning, love? I see Mr Tibbs is pleased you're back."

The old cat opened a lazy eye at the sound of his name before closing it again.

Olivia sat up quickly as her gran placed the tray across her knee. There was so much to say, but where to start?

"Who is Mary Anne Nicholls, Gran?"

Sue Bailey looked down at her granddaughter in amazement.

"Why Olivia, wherever did you pluck that name from?"

It was easy to explain about the old book and the inscription she had found hidden amongst the pages. She decided to keep quiet about the earlier goings-on that morning at the stone circle. She couldn't even be sure that it had really happened, and perhaps it had just been a dream after all?

The older woman sat on the bed while the young girl munched on her toast.

"Well, Olivia, Mary Anne Nicholls was my Grandmother, my mother's mother. That book must have been hers. It's a very old book that eventually became my mother's. I inherited it with a few things, but I never knew about the inscription."

Walking over to the bookcase, she carefully removed the old book, taking care not to tear it any more than it was already. She soon found the inscription.

"The May Queen, I think we have an old photograph of Mary as the May Queen. I'll look it out. She looked a lot like you at your age, you know."

“What about the missing jam tarts, Gran?” Olivia tried not to spit toast over the duvet.

“How on earth do you know that the jam tarts are missing? I only discovered that when I went into the kitchen this morning.”

So the tarts had been missing! Olivia pinched herself hard. Maybe she hadn’t been dreaming after all?

“I was hungry in the night, and I went down to the kitchen to get something to eat. All the tarts had disappeared except for two.”

“Yes, it was quite a mystery this morning; I was beginning to think that you’d eaten them all to yourself. Not that I would have minded. I made them especially for you.”

“I think it might have been the Knave of Hearts,” Olivia mumbled the words quietly, afraid of sounding foolish.

Her gran laughed. “Ha, I suppose he could have been the culprit, but I’m afraid I already know who the thief is, isn’t that right, Mr Tibbs?”

At the mention of his name, Mr Tibbs raised one pointed ear followed by the other.

“Mr Tibbs, surely not?” Olivia stared in disbelief at the old ginger tom, who had started to look uncomfortable.

“I’m afraid so. I found a trail of pastry crumbs and jam that led straight to his basket. No wonder he’s a fat old Puss”.

With as much dignity as he could muster, Mr Tibbs jumped down from the bed and scampered from the room.

“Guilty as charged. Never mind, love, we can make some more today. I know that they’re your favourites. You can help me if you like?”

Olivia smiled, it had been an extraordinary morning, and she had such a lot to tell her gran, but it was difficult to know where to start. Still, that could wait; she had the whole holidays before her, plenty of time to tell her gran all about the May Queen and her strange court at the old stone circle.

“Well, love, what do you think- shall we do some baking later?”

Sitting up, Olivia leaned forward to hug her gran.

“I would like that, gran, I really would. But it would have to be Strawberry Jam Tarts, of course?”

The End

JAM
FLOUR

Would you like to make Strawberry Jam Tarts – just like Olivia and her gran? If so, see the easy-to-follow recipe below.
Always ask an adult to help. Don't forget to wash your hands before you start!

Olivia's Strawberry Jam Tarts

Ingredients

- 300g Plain flour
- 150g Unsalted butter chilled and diced
- 40g Caster sugar
- 1 egg
- Strawberry Jam

Method

- Heat the oven to 190c, 170c fan, gas 5
- Mix the flour, butter, sugar and egg together to make a dough
- Add a splash of water if needed
- Wrap in cling film and refrigerate for 20 minutes
- On a lightly floured base, roll the dough to about a 3mm thickness
- Use a 4" round cutter to cut out 12 round discs
- Place one disc in each whole in the jam tart tin, lightly pressing down the centre to expel any air
- Add a small spoonful of jam to each tart shell
- Bake for approximately 15 minutes till pastry is golden
- CAUTION-EXTREMELY HOT.DO NOT TOUCH THE JAM OR EAT STRAIGHT OUT OF THE OVEN.

- Keep away from the Knave of Hearts wherever possible.

Enjoy x

Printed in Great Britain
by Amazon

69173994R00020